MICHAEL
GARLAND

Christmas
City

a LOOK AGAIN book

Dutton Children's Books

New York

195   5026

To my mother-in-law, Margaret

Copyright © 2002 by Michael Garland
All rights reserved.

CIP Data is available.

Published in the United States 2002 by Dutton Children's Books,
a division of Penguin Putnam Books for Young Readers
345 Hudson Street, New York, New York 10014
www.penguinputnam.com

Printed in Hong Kong
First Edition
ISBN 0-525-46904-4
1 3 5 7 9 10 8 6 4 2

Dear Reader,

This book is a puzzle,
A hide-and-seek game.
Stick with my nephew—
Your path is the same.

Some letters are hiding.
They've something to tell.
Collect and unscramble
To see what they spell.

"The Twelve Days of Christmas"
Is a great Yuletide song.
Find the things that are listed
And you'll never be wrong.

Count angels and cherubs
And candy canes, too.
Find snowmen, elves, reindeer—
They're hiding from you.

Check the book's covers—
The front and the back.
Some things are well hidden,
So try to keep track.

Take a pencil and paper
And carefully look.
Make note of the things
That you find in this book.

My list's at the end—
Take yours and compare.
If the two don't agree,
There's no need to despair.

Look again at these pages,
And as you go through,
You'll find, if you're careful,
My numbers are true.

—Aunt Jeanne

It was Christmas Eve. Tommy was sorting through the last few Christmas cards to arrive when he found one addressed to him. There was a note inside.

Dear Tommy,

Merry Christmas! Good cheer!
The best of the season!
Come meet me at once—
There's no time for a reason!

You'll find a cab waiting.
Enjoy the nice ride.
I'll count all the minutes
Till you're by my side.

—Aunt Jeanne

Tommy put on his hat and coat and walked out into the snowy night. Sure enough, there was a yellow taxi waiting for him, buried in snow up to its fenders. The driver was a strange little man who had to stand on the seat to see out the windshield. He didn't answer when Tommy said hello. He just smiled and handed Tommy a note.

But before Tommy could read it, the quiet night was broken by the roar of the engine. This was no ordinary cab! Tommy gasped as it lifted off the ground into the air.

The rocket cab streaked across the sky. Tommy looked out as they soared through snowflakes and then past stars. It seemed to him they had flown halfway across the world by the time the cab started to descend toward a cluster of glowing lights in the distance. As they got closer, Tommy could see that the lights belonged to a glittering city. He remembered Aunt Jeanne's note, now crumpled in his hand. He smoothed it out and read it.

You'll soon reach a place
As strange as it's pretty.
It holds many secrets—
It's called Christmas City.

The cab touched down and glided along an ice canal before skidding to a stop. Tommy got out and walked toward the entrance to the city. His eyes scanned the crowd for Aunt Jeanne, but instead he spotted a note speared to the tip of an icicle.

Welcome! Come in!

Here it's Christmas all year!

If you find the Grand Palace,

Then I will be near.

Tommy entered the city through the stone arches, determined to find the Grand Palace—and his aunt.

Tommy had never been to such a beautiful place. Not a single car could be seen— just sleighs darting about, their bells ringing in the air. The people were strangely dressed, and a few odd creatures plodded through the snowy streets. Tommy bought a candied apple, but before he could take a bite, he noticed a note stuck to the red coating.

Enjoy your nice treat
And just wander around.
Fill up your ears
With that quaint Christmas sound.

Before Tommy had gone too far, he remembered that he needed to shop for Aunt Jeanne's Christmas present. He had no idea what to get or where to get it. Then he saw a note sticking out of a snowdrift.

Around the next corner,
There's a marvelous store.
Shopping for me
Is a game, not a chore.

Tommy entered the crowded store and looked around in confusion. He didn't know where to begin to find a gift for Aunt Jeanne. He put his hands in his pockets. Someone had placed a note in one of them.

Don't flutter around
Like an angel with wings.
Ask at the counter—
They'll show you some things.

Tommy made his way to the counter and told one of the little elves that he was looking for a gift for his Aunt Jeanne. An elf winked and handed Tommy a note.

What has a face
But doesn't have eyes?
It's the perfect gift,
And just the right size!

Be on your way.
There's more you must see:
A magnificent splendor—
The new Christmas tree!

ommy selected the gift, and the elves wrapped it up for him. Then he left the store and followed the directions to the Christmas tree. Even from a distance, Tommy could tell it was the most fantastic tree in the whole world. Right away he noticed one particular branch laden with golden ornaments. He spotted a note dangling below them.

The secret, you'll guess,
To winning this game
Is to write the first letter
Of each object's name.

Unjumble the letters—
I'll tell you the reason:
This word is the heart
Of the whole Christmas season.

When your answer's complete,
This test's at an end.
The courtyard is next
If you've more time to spend.

When Tommy reached the courtyard, he was dazzled by the ice sculptures that towered over him. As he stood gazing up, a breeze blew a note past his nose. Tommy snatched it before it could blow away.

These statues are cold,
But you have a warm heart.
You'll find me soon, Tommy—
You've made a great start.

Look over your shoulder.
The Grand Palace beckons.
A hop, skip, and jump
Get you there in ten seconds.

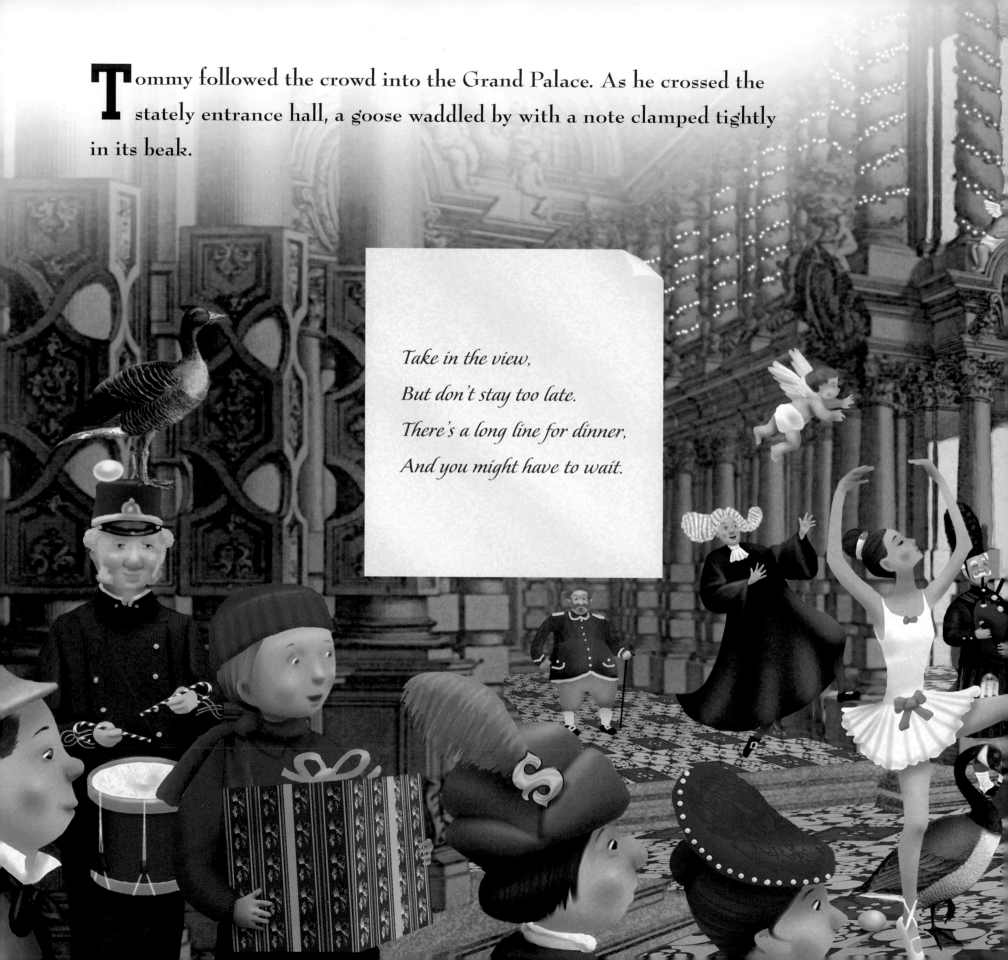

Tommy followed the crowd into the Grand Palace. As he crossed the stately entrance hall, a goose waddled by with a note clamped tightly in its beak.

Take in the view,
But don't stay too late.
There's a long line for dinner,
And you might have to wait.

When Tommy entered the dining room, the wonderful aromas made him hungry. He waited on the buffet line to fill up his plate. When he had piled it high with his favorite foods, he looked around the room for an empty seat. They all seemed to be taken. Tommy glanced down at his plate and noticed there was a note sticking out of his double-decker sandwich.

Your plate is now loaded.
There's still one free chair.
A trip through this maze
Will take you right there!

Enjoy the big feast—
It's a fine, tasty treat.
Next there's music and dancing
To tickle your feet.

The ballroom down the hall was filled with music and people in fancy clothes. Before Tommy could take two steps, he was dragged out onto the dance floor and twirled round and round by a lady in a long dress. When the music stopped, she thanked Tommy and put a note in his hand.

Have a good time—
Just dance yourself silly.
Keep moving around,
And you'll never get chilly.

When you've had enough dancing
And you'd like to see me,
Climb right up the stairs.
That's the place where I'll be.

Tommy pushed his way through the crowd and bounded up the steps until he reached a huge door. There was a note tied to the knob.

Please open the door.
You've come to the end!
There's someone to meet—
He's my special new friend.

Dear Reader • Now that you have reached the end of this book, have you found everything there was to find? Don't forget to look on the title page and the front and back covers! • There are 18 angels, 26 cherubs, 35 candy canes, 36 tiny elves, and 17 snowmen. • Did you see the hidden Christmas greetings in 10 different languages? Spanish: "Feliz Navidad." French: "Joyeux Noël." Portuguese: "Boas Festas." Italian: "Buon Natale." Lithuanian: "Linksmu Kaledu." Hawaiian: "Mele Kalikimaka." Bulgarian: "Tchestita Koleda." Icelandic: "Gledileg Jól." Irish: "Nollaig Shona Dhuit." Danish: "Gladelig Jul." • Did you find Santa's eight reindeer? (Some are hidden, and some are in plain sight.) Look for their names, too: Donder, Dancer, Prancer, Vixen, Comet, Blitzen, Cupid, and Dasher. • Were you able to spot all the hidden letters that spell out MERRY CHRISTMAS? This greeting can also be found upside down and backwards on the back cover. • On the Christmas tree page, Tommy uses the first letter of each gold object's name to spell out the word P-E-A-C-E (Pineapple, Eye, Anchor, Catfish, Elephant) • Everything listed in the carol "The Twelve Days of Christmas" appears in this book. Did you find 12 drummers drumming, 11 pipers piping, 10 lords a-leaping, 9 ladies dancing, 8 maids a-milking, 7 swans a-swimming, 6 geese a-laying, 5 gold rings, 4 calling birds, 3 French hens, 2 turtledoves, and a partridge in a pear tree? • Come back to Christmas City anytime—the gates are always open. • —Aunt Jeanne